This TWO HOOTS
book belongs to:

# For Dexter and Jessica

With giggle-filled memories of my Uncle Peter Beanbrain

Huge thanks to my editor Suzanne Carnell and my designer Sharon King-Chai
for their warmth and encouragement . . . and for always listening. It's been a hoot!

First published 2017 by Two Hoots
an imprint of Pan Macmillan
20 New Wharf Road, London N1 9RR
Associated companies throughout the world www.panmacmillan.com
ISBN 978-1-5098-1398-8 (HB) ISBN 978-1-5098-1417-6 (PB)
Text and illustrations copyright © Zehra Hicks 2017. Moral rights asserted.

1 3 5 7 9 8 6 4 2
A CIP catalogue record for this book is available from the British Library.
Printed in Spain
The illustrations in this book were created using monoprint, pen and ink, pencil,
pastel, watercolour and collage . . . and a bit of Photoshop.

www.twohootsbooks.com

Zehra Hicks

# GIRAFFE AND FROG

TWO HOOTS

Giraffe and Frog were going to the beach.
Frog knew the way.

Err, Giraffe?
I think it's
this way.

But Giraffe wasn't listening.

Come along, Frog.
Follow me.

But Giraffe?
I've been
there
before.

I've got
a map!

But Giraffe wasn't listening.

Err, Giraffe?
This isn't the beach!
The beach has sand.
We can't build
sandcastles in a field!

Ah yes, of course, sand.
I knew that.
Leave it to me!

And off Giraffe went. In the wrong direction.

But Giraffe wasn't listening.

Err, Giraffe?
This is NOT the beach!
The beach is by the sea.
We can't swim in the
middle of a desert!

Ah yes, of course, sea.
I knew that.
    Leave it to me!

Giraffe set off again, still going the wrong way.

But Giraffe wasn't listening.

Here we are!

GIRAFFE!
THIS IS NOT
THE BEACH!
BEANBRAIN!

Pardon?

What did you say, Frog?

At last you're
listening!
Come on, let's go -
I know the way.

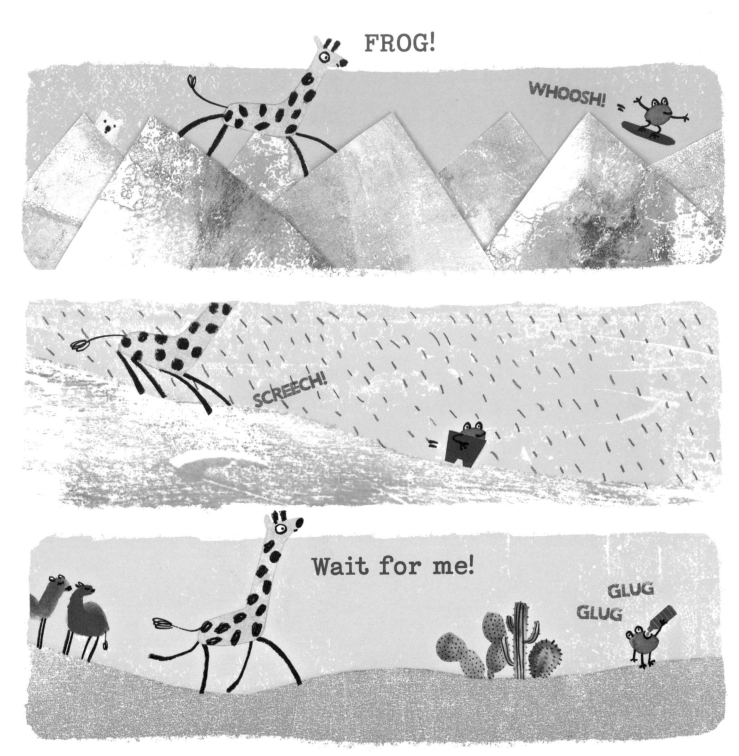

Not far now!

Here we are!

BEACH

**THIS**
is the beach!

Ah, yes,
of course.
I knew that.

There was sand . . .

and sea . . .

and the two friends had a wonderful time together.

I'm sorry I didn't listen to you, Frog.

That's okay, Giraffe.
I'm sorry I called you
Beanbrain.

I know,
let's have
an ice cream!

Frog knew the way.

But Giraffe?

Giraffe wasn't listening.

**Zehra Hicks** is an illustrator, writer,
designer, mother, cyclist, and chocolate-lover.
She has a unique approach to illustration,
not limited to pencils and paper and paint.
Zehra has been known to use sticks, bamboo
and potatoes to create her books, and
sometimes her two children help, too.
Zehra almost never stops moving –
always in the right direction, of course!